HOLY MOSES!

Pop cantata for unison voices and piano

words and music by

CHRIS HAZELL

NOVELLO PUBLISHING LIMITED
8/9 Frith Street, London W1V 5TZ

Order No: NOV 200148

COMPOSER'S NOTE

I have deliberately kept dynamics and phrasing to a minimum to allow as much freedom in interpretation as possible. Similarly, the voice groupings are merely guides, any part being suitable for solo, small or large group singing depending upon availability or choice.

The piano part is complete in itself, but any additional instruments (particularly bass and drums) will improve the performance. The chord symbols do not always give complete harmonies. In any bar where there is no symbol the guitar should remain *tacet*.

The Bible passages are optional, but, where used, should be taken from the Standard Revised Version.

DURATION ABOUT 22 MINUTES

Parts for Bass and Drums are available on sale.

COVER DESIGN BY ROBERTO ZAMARIN

To Jennifer Paull

HOLY MOSES!

Pop Cantata for Unison voices and Piano

Words and Music by
CHRIS HAZELL

Exodus 2, vv. 1–4

1 THE BULRUSH SONG

C
Gsus
G7
Csus
C
is. Well what is it that is float-ing in a front - door mat?
C7
F
C
F
2
C
F
Did it bark? Did it miaow? It's a
8
Ab
Bb
Fsus
F
C7
F
ve - ry fun-ny noise that it's mak - ing now. It's a dog, it's a
8
A7
Dm
C
F
Cmaj7
cat, it's a bear, it's a bat. Ho - ly Mo - ses! It's a

3
Fmaj7
Dm7
F
Em7
A7
F
ba - by. You don't know how right you are! Who's this com-ing in a
Bb
Bbm
F
Bb
Fsus
F
long white gown, Look-ing like the Queen of She-ba for a night on the town? It's the
Phar-aoh's daugh-ter and look what she's done, She's tak-en up the ba-by and is
4
call-ing it 'son'.
8

PHARAOH
FULL
Ab
Bb
'What's this_ you've got?' Said the Phar-aoh as he stooped to see the
Fsus
F
C7
PHARAOH
F
A7
Dm
ti - ny tot._ 'He must stay_ now he's here, We could do_with the
C
Gsus
G7
5
Csus
C
dear, For E - gyp-tian mum-mies can't ex-ist with - out a son.
C7
F
C
Gm
C
F
You've got_ a nerve To a -

Ab
Bb
Fsus
F
C7
F
dopt a lit-tle ba-by that was born_ to serve.
Still I've got_ to ad-
8
A7
Dm
C
6
Gsus
G7
mit That I like_him a bit,
E-ven though his mo-ther must have been an
Csus
C
C7
F
C
F
C
Is-rael-ite._
We must find_
8
F
Ab
Bb
Fsus
F
him a nurse, 'Cos to fos-ter such a child would be a ter-ri-ble curse.
8

C7 F A7 Dm 7 C
This young wo - man will do. What's she say - ing to you?'
F
MOSES' MOTHER Cmaj7 Fmaj7 FULL Dm7 F
'Ho - ly Mo - ses! It's my ba - by.' You don't know how right you
Cmaj7 F Cmaj7 Fmaj7
are! 'Ho - ly Mo - ses! It's my ba - by.' You don't
Dm7 F 8 Csus C C7 F Csus C
know how right you are!

Exodus 2, vv. 11-12,15

2 THE PROMISE

A
B
B dim
Sud-den-ly came_ on a burn-ing bush Won - der'd what he'd
E
A
D
E
E
A
found. Out of it came the voice of God,_ say-ing
D
D
E
11
A
'This is Ho-ly ground Take off your shoes, Mo-ses
B
B dim
A
come up here; Don't be scared of me.

F#m B7 D E D Am D7
I will give you pow-er to free my peo - ple.
12
Mo-ses you'll free all my peo - ple from Phar-aoh's hand,
Leav-ing be-hind you the blood on E -
gyp-tian sand.
A B
Don't be a - fraid of the job you've got,

13
B dim
E A
D E
I'll help all I can.
Phar-aoh will have to
E A
D
D E
list-en when I un-fold my mas-ter plan.
A
B
B dim
You will es-cape to the pro-mised land,
Put your trust in me.
A
14 F♯m B7
D E D
I will give you pow-er to free my
Am D7 Am D7
peo-ple, my peo-ple.'

Exodus 3, vv. 10, 19-20

3 MOSES' MAGIC BOX

16
G D Bm7 E7 G D
snake out of an - y old broom. Watch me a-maze all his wise old men.
G Am7 G C7
What will they think of God's pow-er when The Is-rael-ites raise a
F G F♯m Em7 A G A Bsus B
loud 'A - men!' We'll show the E - gyp - tians who are mas-ters then.
17
D Am7 G
I'll turn in-to blood the wa-ters of the Nile By touch-ing it once with my
Drums only, if available, for this bar.

D
D
Am7
rod. I'll make all the ri - vers and foun-tains vile; I'll
G
D
Bm7
E7
show you the pow - er of God. Watch me a - maze all his
18
G
D
G
Am7
wise old men. What will they think of God's pow - er when The
G
C7
F
G
F♯m
Em
A
Is-rael-ites raise a loud 'A - men!' We'll show the E - gyp - tians who are

G A Bsus B
mas - ters then. _
D
Still you re - fuse _ to set my
Drums only, if available, for this bar.
19
Am7
peo-ple free; It's
G
trou-ble you're go - ing to
D
get. The
D
Lord will be an - gry just you
Am7
wait and see; _ You
G
ain't seen the last _ of me
D
yet.
Bm7 E7
Watch me a - maze _ all his
G D
wise old men. _

20
G
Am7
G
C7
What will they think of God's pow-er when The Is-rael-ites raise a
F G F♯m
Em7
A
G A Bsus B
loud 'A-men!' We'll show the E-gyp-tians who are mas-ters then.
Drums only, if available, for this bar
D
G D E D
A
Con-jur-ing tricks right be-fore your eyes, Con-jur-ing tricks right be-
C G A
Am7
21
Am7 D C
senza rall.
fore your eyes, Con-jur-ing tricks right be-fore your eyes.

4 THE PLAGUE ON YOU

G
Em
Am
plague of frogs in-side your house, You'll soon wish you were dead.
F
D
G
Gm
They'll get in cup-boards, o-vens, wells, And
23
D
Bm
G
A
Bm
ev - en in your bed. If you still won't
Bm
G
D
G
let them go, God will send a plague of flies.

Bm
Bm
Em
G
Phar - aoh let my peo - ple go Be - fore some - bo - dy
8
C
D
24
G
Am
dies.
Plagues up - on the E -
3
8
G
F
Dsus
C
gyp - tians; Phar - aoh look out, 'cos you're in for a scare. Be -
G
Am
G
F
ware of Mo - ses' pre - dic - tions Phar - aoh, keep the Is - rael - ites out of your

25
Dsus D G Em
hair. A plague of lo - custs eats — your crops, All
Am F D
green things dis - ap - pear. The dust you'll eat be - neath
G Gm D Bm G A
— your feet, The curse of God is here. —
Bm Bm G
26
D G
If you still won't let them go, Fire and hail will hide the sun.

Bm Bm Em G
Might - y Phar - aoh, you've been warned, There's worse that's still to
C D G Am
come. Plagues up-on the E -
27
G F Dsus C
gyp-tians; Phar-aoh look out, 'cos you're in for a scare. Be -
G Am C F
ware of Mo-ses' pre - dic-tions Phar-aoh, keep the Is-rael-ites now, the
F F G Am G
Is-rael-ites now, the Is-rael-ites now if you dare.

Exodus 11, v. 1

5 ANGEL OF DEATH

Em
F
Bm
This is the night of the Pass-o-ver feast: Ang-el of Death, pass by.
30
C7
C7
Find a lamb that is one year old;
Take it out of your fa-ther's fold;

Em
F
Bm
Em
Roast it with herbs and un - leav-n'd bread, Eat it to - night or you
F
Bm
31
may be dead: An-gel of Death, pass by.
Em
C
F#7

Em
C
32
F#7
Em
3
F
Bm
Em
F
Bm
PHARAOH
33
I am the Phar-aoh of this
C7
C7
place.
An-gel of Death, come and show your

C7
C7
Em
F
Bm
face.
Mo-ses has told me a great big lie;
Em
34
F
Bm
On-ly the peo-ple I choose will die:
An-gel of Death, pass
by!
FULL
C7
C7
Phar-aoh's son ly-ing on the floor;

35
C7
C7
Cold and life-less be - side the door.
Em
F
Bm
Em
Phar-aoh comes in, sees him ly-ing there; An-gel of Death fly-ing
F
Bm
PHARAOH
through the air: Ho - ly Mo - ses! It's my
36
ba - by.

Exodus 13, v. 18
14, vv. 5-6

6 THE CHASE

Cm
Cm
F7
Fm
God of our peo - ple help me run, This
Cm
Ab Bb
Cm
F
dust and sand has made me blind.
His char - iots
Bb
Bbdim
F
Bb
go so fast,
His sol - diers are so cruel.
39
F
Bb
Bbdim
Ab
I don't know if I'll last,
And nei - ther does my

G7
Cm
F7
Fm
mule. Char-iot wheels of rac-ing doom, The
Cm
Ab
Cm
Cm
sun is bla-zing hot.
Are we all going to
F7
Fm
40
Cm
Ab
Bb
Cm
die so soon? We've been through such an aw-ful lot.

41
Cm
F7
Fm
Cuck - ling hens and bleat - ing lambs, To
Cm
Ab
Cm
beat them's so un - kind._
Cm
If we don't go much
F7
Fm
Cm
Ab Bb Cm
fas - ter though, We'll have to leave them all be - hind._

42
F Bb Bbdim F
They're getting very close, Just hear the horses
Bb F Bb
neigh. I'm really fright-en'd now,— We'll
Bbdim Ab G7 Cm
ne-ver get a-way. God of our peo-ple
F7 Fm Cm Ab Cm
where've you gone? I think you've left us all.—
3

43
Cm
F7
Fm
Cm
Why don't you come and help us, Lord? Or don't you want to
Ab Bb Cm
Am Em Am Em
F C F C
hear our call? What's that glist-'ning in the dis - tance?
Dm Am Dm B7
E
E7
A
Ho - ly Mo - ses! It's the
Dm Am Dm Am
44
Dm Am Dm Am
Bb F Bb F
Red Sea, And it does - n't look that

Gm Dm Gm Dm G Cm
far! How are we going to
F7 Fm Cm Ab Cm
get a-cross? We have-n't got a boat.
Cm F7 Fm 45 Cm
Are we sup-posed to swim it all? 'Cos I won't make it,
Ab Bb Cm F Bb
I can't float. What's Mo-ses do-ing now? He's

B♭dim F B♭ F
lift - ing up his rod. The seas are
B♭ B♭ dim A♭ G7
fall - ing back, He's got the pow'r of God.
46
Cm F7 Fm Cm A♭
Now we are going to get a - cross, The Lord has heard our call.
Cm Cm F7 Fm
Hur-ry to reach the o - ther side, I'm

Cm
Ab Bb Cm
Am Em Am Em
wor - ried that the sea will fall.
Look, the sea has
3
3
47
F C F C
Dm Am Dm B7
E E7
fall - en on them.
Ho - ly
3
3
3
3
A
Dm Am Dm Am
Dm Am Dm Am
Mo - ses! They're all drown - ing!
We've es -
poco rall.
Bb B C C#
D Ebm
caped the Phar - aoh's men!

a tempo
48
Cm
F7
Fm
God has helped Mo - ses save us all_ From
Drums only,
if available, for this bar
Cm
Ab
Cm
Cm
might - y Phar-aoh's hand._
Now we are free to
F7
Fm
Cm
Ab Bb
Cm
tra - vel on_ Un - til we reach the pro-mised land.
Cm
F7
Fm
49
Ab Bb
Cm(9)

Exodus 14, vv. 30–31

7 FREEDOM

51
C
The Is-rael-ites have got free-dom. Free-dom from the
f
Bb Dm Csus C Bb Dm
ir-on hand of the Phar-aoh. We can do what we like_ where
Csus C
we go, Thanks to Mo-ses. Mo-ses bought us all free-dom.
52
Bb
Pil-lars_ of

Ab Cm Bbsus Bb Ab Cm
smoke to guide us by day-time, And a pil-lar of fire_ by the
Bbsus Bb Ab Cm Bbsus Bb
night-time. But where's Mo-ses? God's
53
Ab Cm Bbsus Bb Ab Cm
called him up_ to the moun-tain; It's be-cause of him_we've got
Bbsus Bb
free-dom. Mo-ses has brought us all free-

8 TEN OF THE BEST

D G G Bb+ Bm7 Em7
you must all do As you go on your way
G C C
57
Gm A7
to day. Take them down with great care,
F#m Dsus Am Bbdim. Dsus D Gm7
Take them back to your clan. I shall watch;
C7
58
F Bb Eb D G
Mo-ses, be - ware, Keep them as well as I know you can

59
G Bb+ Bm7 Em7 G D F
As you go on your way to - day.
D G A Bm A G
Here's the first law, Mo-ses, you must love me; Don't make my
60
A Bm A B7 Em7 G
i-mage from out of a tree; Don't take my name in vain.
poco rall.
a tempo
D G Am7 G A Bm
Re - mem-ber the Sab-bath, for then you must

61
A G A Bm A B7
rest; Be good to your pa-rents and you will be blessed; Mo -
rall.
62
a tempo
Em G D Am7 Dsus Gm
ses, don't kill. You must be true
Gm A7 F#m Dsus Am Bb dim
to your wife, You must learn not to steal.
63
Dsus D Gm7 C7 F Bb Eb
Don't tell lies, don't let en - vy Rule your life, and

D G G Bb+ Bm7 Em7
you'll be o - kay As you go on your way;
64
G Bb+ Bm7 Em7 G Bb+
make sure you pray As you go
Bm7 Em7 G D F D F
on your way to - day.
65
D F D F D F D F D F D F
D C Em
Mo-ses brought us re - li - gion!
ff
8

Deuteronomy 7, vv. 12–13
31, vv. 1–2, 7–8

9 MOSES' FAREWELL

Ab
Fm
Bbm
Eb7
Milk and ho - ney flow Where my peo - ple
67
Cm
Fm
Bbm
go. See them pass-ing on their way, But here I'll
Db
Gm7
C7
F
C
Dm
stay; I'll ne-ver know... Now his job is done,
Gm
Em7
A7
Dm
F7
He is like the sun; Hav - ing walked a-cross the

68
Dm
Gm
Cm
Gm7
C7
sky His light be-gins to die, But the stor-y's just be - gun. Re -
F
Eb
F
Eb7
F
Eb
mem - ber what God's done for you So trust him like I learned to
Dm7
G7
Cm7
Ab
Gm
Gm7
C7
do. He gave you the chance — Take it with both hands; You'll
Ab
Gm
69
Gm7
C7
find his pro-mis-es come true.

F C Dm Gm
MOSES
You are not a - lone, This I hope I've
Em7 A7 Dm F7 Dm
shown. Now I've seen the pro-mised land, I'm in Je-ho-vah's
70
Gm Cm Gm7 Gm7 C7
hand... Re -
F Eb F Eb7 F Eb
mem - ber what God's done for you So trust him like I learned to

Dm7 G7 Cm7 A♭ Gm Gm7 C7
do. He gave you the chance — Take it with both hands; You'll
A♭ Gm Gm7 C7
find his pro-mi-ses come true.
71 F C Dm Gm
ISRAELITES I
Mo - ses has shown us that we're not a -
ISRAELITES II {We
MOSES {You} are not a - lone, This {we
I} know {you've
I've}
71

Printed and bound in Great Britain by
Caligraving Limited Thetford Norfolk